W9-AAH-877

Spunky's™ Circus Adventure
Copyright © 1999
Global Television Syndications
Christian Broadcasting Network

Published by Bethany House Publishers. Based on character and story from
Spunky's Diary by Janette Oke. This story was adapted for television by Patrick Granleese
and modified for print by Sue & Lorianne Wilkinson. Illustrated by Elizabeth Gatt,
Sue Wilkinson, and Holly Lennox. Art Direction by Angela Ward Costello,
Lindy Lindstrom, Sue Wilkinson, Dynomight Cartoons, and CBN Animation.

Printed in Italy.

Library of Congress CIP Data applied for

ISBN 0-7642-2194-9

This book belongs to

_____

Based on character and story by

JANETTE OKE

Spunky's

Circus Adventure

Spunky has hidden his duck somewhere on each double page. Can you find it?

A surprise!

That's what
Mr. Dobson had
promised Mark and Spunky
at breakfast. Spunky wagged his
tail and looked around. Whatever
the surprise was, it must be big. The
whole town had come to see it.

Boom! Toot! Spunky's ears perked up.
Two clowns came into view,
carrying a wide banner.

Behind them marched the band that was making all the noise.

"Look, Spunky, the circus is in town!" shouted Mark.

Mr. Dobson pointed. "There's my old friend Mr. Callahan. He's the ringmaster. That's his daughter, Julie, beside him."

An elephant with huge feet plodded past Spunky.

"Elephants! Lions! Ostriches! Wow, this is going to be great!" exclaimed Mark. "And look, monkeys!"

"Doggie, wanna see Frankie's best trick?" called a monkey.

Frankie snatched a key from his trainer's pocket.

Unlocking the door of his cage, he dashed out and leapt right onto Mark's shoulder.

"Nice hat. Frankie wear?" The monkey grabbed Mark's hat and scampered off.

Spunky bolted after Frankie but soon lost him.

"Boo!" shouted Frankie from behind.

Spunky jumped straight up—into the arms of a woman watching the parade.

"Hee hee! Nice jump," said Frankie.

"Give me back that hat," barked Spunky.

Mark and the Dobsons finally caught up with Spunky and Frankie at Mr. Callahan's wagon. Laughing, Mr. Callahan handed Frankie over to his trainer. Patting Spunky's head, Mr. Callahan said, "I was expecting to see you folks, but not quite so soon."

That night, Spunky and Mark sat under the huge canvas big top. Spunky felt dizzy trying to watch everything.

Clowns sprayed each other with hoses. Trapeze artists flew through the air. The lion tamer stuck his head way inside a lion's mouth. It was a great show.

Spunky didn't think he'd ever seen Mark so happy . . . but the best was still to come. Tomorrow, Mr. Callahan said, Mark and Spunky could work at the circus!

Back home, Mark said his bedtime prayers. "And thank you, Jesus, for a great day at the circus. I promise to do my best when I work for Mr. Callahan tomorow. Amen."

Bright and early the next morning, Mark and Spunky knocked at Mr. Callahan's door. *I hope we don't have to brush the lions*, thought Spunky.

Mr. Callahan sent Julie to feed the monkeys. Then he turned to Mark. "I have a special job for you," he said.

Mr. Callahan handed Mark a pointed stick and a sack. "Wow, a lion-taming stick, Spunky!" Mark shouted.

But Mr. Callahan showed Mark how to use the stick to pick up trash. "I run a clean outfit here, Mark," said the ringmaster.

"Yes, sir!" said Mark. "I'll pick up every last bit of trash."

"Good. And be sure to keep an eye on Spunky."

Spunky and Mark got to
work and soon had a full bag.

"No job is too big if you are
just willing to work hard,"
Mark told Spunky.

Just then they came to the monkey cage and saw Julie.

"I'm bored," she announced. "Tie Spunky's leash to the cage, and let's go on some rides."

"Well . . . okay," said Mark. "Just for a bit. Then I should get back to work." After all, Julie was the ringmaster's daughter. It must be okay.

Julie stuffed the last of the old bananas into
Mark's trash bag. She didn't feel Frankie
lifting the key from her pocket. She and Mark
headed for the midway.

Creeeeak. The cage door swung open behind Spunky. Out leapt Frankie and his friends. They went right for Mark's sack to get those bananas. Garbage flew everywhere.

"Hey! My master worked hard cleaning that up," Spunky growled.

"Bananas all gone," cried Frankie. But he soon thought of more mischief.

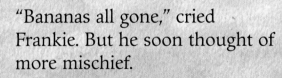

Creeeeak. Spunky heard another cage door opening, and another. A bear thundered past. Then an ostrich flounced by.

Yikes! The ground shook as the elephants stomped over Spunky, who hid his head in his paws.

Snap! The leash broke, and Spunky raced after the monkeys.

Spunky screeched to a halt. He looked up into the face of a VERY large kitty.

ROARRR!

Spunky turned and ran. "Help, help, help!" he yelped.

"We get help!" screeched Frankie.

Dust flew in the air. Animals ran every which way. Flip, flop, *thud*, *whoosh!* Dodging elephants, barking at seals, Spunky raced about, with the lion in hot pursuit.

At last Spunky paused, gasping for breath. Just as the lion was going to pounce, the lion tamer appeared and shouted, "Back to your cage!"

Whew! thought Spunky. *That was close!*

Mr. Callahan and the Dobsons
ran up. Mr. Callahan hollered,
"What's going on here?
Get these animals into
their cages!"

The trainers raced around putting the animals back.
Except for Frankie, that is. He was prancing about
with another stolen hat.

Spunky grabbed the hat and ran for the monkey's cage. He ran right in—and so did Frankie. The trainer quickly slammed the door, then opened it just enough to let Spunky slip back out.

Peace descended on the circus.

Just then Spunky spied Mark and Julie getting off a ride. Mark rushed over to Spunky as Julie ran to her dad.

Mr. Callahan was standing, hands on hips, gazing at the mess. "Who is responsible for all this?" he demanded. "Who let the animals out?"

Julie, who had discovered by then that her key was missing, looked up. "Mark said he didn't like the job you gave him. I'll bet he took the key and let the animals out," she told her dad.

"I never did any such thing!" shouted Mark.

"Well, the trash didn't walk by itself," snapped Mr. Callahan. "And what about Spunky? I suppose you didn't take your eyes off him, either?"

"Mark," said Mr. Dobson, "what does God say in the Bible about honesty?"

"He says I shouldn't lie," Mark answered. "But I didn't lie. I did leave Spunky, that's true, and I shouldn't have. But I didn't let the animals out."

Spunky had an idea. He could prove Mark was telling the truth. *Woof, woof!*

"Frankie, bet you can't do your trick again," Spunky barked.

Frankie leaned over and plucked Mr. Callahan's keys from his pocket.

"That's it! Frankie took Julie's key," Mark exclaimed.

"He must be right, Dad," said Julie. "I lost my key and was afraid you'd be mad, so I blamed Mark. I'm sorry, Mark. Can you forgive me?"

"Sure, Julie. Thanks for telling the truth," said Mark.

He turned to Mark. "I'm sorry I blamed you. Let me make it up to you. Tonight you will have the best view in the big top."

Wow! The center ring! Spunky gazed around. Mark clapped his hands. Oops, Spunky was supposed to be a lion!

"Roarrrr!" Spunky tossed his mane. Mark waved his arms and pointed at the drum. "Up!" he called.

Spunky could barely hear Mark over the roar of the crowd. *I wonder if Mark's head will fit in my mouth,* he thought. He stretched his mouth wider and wider . . . and the crowd went wild!

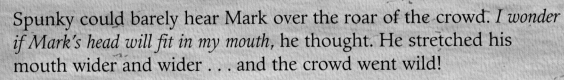